Sivu's Six Wishes

Sivu's Six Wishes was edited, designed, and published in 2010 by
Frances Lincoln Children's Books
4 Torriano Mews, Torriano Avenue, London NW5 2RZ U.K.

This edition published in 2010 by agreement with Frances Lincoln Limited by
Eerdmans Books for Young Readers
an imprint of Wm. B. Eerdmans Publishing Co.
2140 Oak Industrial Dr. NE
Grand Rapids, Michigan 49505
P.O. Box 163, Cambridge CB3 9PU U.K.

www.eerdmans.com/youngreaders

Manufactured at C&C Offset Printing Co., Ltd. in Shenzhen, Guangdong, China in April 2010, first edition

10 11 12 13 14 15 16 17   9 8 7 6 5 4 3 2 1

Library of Congress Cataloging-in-Publication Data
Daly, Jude.
Sivu's six wishes : a Taoist tale / written and illustrated by Jude Daly.
p. cm.
Summary: Sivu, an African stonecarver, is not paid well for his work, but through his wishes to become
more powerful and live as different people, like the mayor, and things, like the wind, he discovers where real power lies.
ISBN 978-0-8028-5369-1 (alk. paper)
[1. Contentment — Fiction. 2. Wishes — Fiction. 3. Stone carvers — Fiction. 4. Taoism — Fiction. 5. Africa — Fiction.] I. Title.
PZ.D16958Siv 2010
[E]--dc22
2010001619

Illustrated with acrylics

Sivu's Six Wishes

A Taoist Tale

Retold and illustrated by

Jude Daly

Eerdmans Books for Young Readers

Grand Rapids, Michigan • Cambridge, U.K.

Sivu was a stonemason who created extraordinary things
from stone. Before he began carving, he would stare into
the rock until he saw a shape in it. Then slowly, slowly,
he would chip away with his hammer and chisel.

People would watch in awe as he coaxed an animal or person out of the lifeless rock. He sold whatever he created, but he never made much money, and he grew bitter and disappointed.

One day, Sivu was carving a statue for a rich businessman's wife. It was hard work, and while he rested, he looked at the businessman's grand house and thought, "How powerful that man must be!"

And the more he thought about it, the more envious he became — until he wished he could BE the businessman.

Suddenly, mysteriously, and to his great surprise, Sivu WAS the businessman. What a life! With the snap of his fingers, he would demand a meal in the middle of the night. With the next snap, he would declare that a shipment of wool was too woolly.

On and on he would argue, until the defeated wool trader
settled for a lower price. Sivu had more power and possessions
than he could ever want, but now his life was miserable
because everyone disliked him.

One day, coming home after arguing about some oranges that he said were too orange, Sivu was held up by a procession. It was the mayor and his officials, and everyone had to stop while the procession went by. As Sivu waited and watched, he thought, "How powerful that mayor must be!"

And the more he thought about it, the more envious he became — until he wished he could BE the mayor.

Suddenly, mysteriously, and to his great surprise,

Sivu WAS the mayor. What a life! Wherever he went,

people stepped aside for him.

He was promised this and promised that if only he would approve this and approve that. He had the power to ruin people, and they all hated him.

One day, Sivu was opening the new botanical gardens. It was so hot that the people and the flowers were wilting under the sun, but Sivu went on with his speech. When he finished, everyone clapped and cheered, while he gazed up at the sun shining proudly in the sky. As Sivu gazed, he thought, "How powerful that sun must be!"

And the more he thought about it, the more envious he became — until he wished he could BE the sun!

Suddenly, mysteriously, and to his great surprise,

Sivu WAS the sun. What a life! He shone down

fiercely on the new botanical gardens and the farmlands.

He scorched the fields and dried up the rivers.

Soon the country was gripped by drought,

and everybody cursed him.

One day, a huge rain cloud
moved between Sivu and
the Earth. He tried to burn
it away, but the cloud
blocked out his rays,
and the Earth started to
cool. Sivu thought, "How
powerful that rain cloud
must be!"

And the more he thought
about it, the more envious
he became — until he
wished he could BE a rain
cloud.

Suddenly, mysteriously, and to his great surprise,
Sivu WAS a rain cloud. What a life! He flooded
the fields and turned roads into rivers.

The waters rose, forcing everyone to leave their homes.
And as they waded through the rising water, people
shouted and swore at Sivu.

One day, Sivu felt himself being swept along by the wind. He went on raining, but the rain fell further and further out to sea. As Sivu's torrent turned to a trickle and then dried up, he thought, "How powerful that wind must be!"

And the more he thought about it, the more envious he became — until he wished he could BE the wind.

Suddenly, mysteriously, and to his great surprise,
Sivu WAS the wind. What a life! He blew hats
and kites away and ripped up trees by their roots.

He even blew a great ship off course.
Nothing escaped his force, and everyone
hurled insults at him.

One day, Sivu blew against something that would not move. No matter how hard he blew, he couldn't move it. It was an enormous rock. As Sivu blew around it, he thought, "How powerful that rock must be!"

And the more he thought about it, the more envious he became — until he wished he could BE a rock.

Suddenly, mysteriously, and to his great surprise,
Sivu WAS a rock. What a life! He was bigger
and more powerful than anything else on earth.

But as he stood there, he heard banging,

then more banging.

It was a hammer pounding a chisel.

Sivu felt his shape being changed. "What could be more powerful than me?" he thought.

And while Sivu thought, far below him people watched in awe as a stonemason brought the rock to life.

About the story

Sivu's Six Wishes is a retelling of the Taoist tale "The Stone Cutter."
Tao (or Dao), meaning "path" or "way," is the name given to a variety of related
Chinese philosophical and religious traditions and concepts.
The Three Jewels of the Tao are compassion, moderation, and humility.
It is a peaceful religion.

Folk stories travel well, not only throughout the world but also
through time. In keeping with this tradition, *Sivu's Six Wishes*
is set in the present, but Sivu the stonemason
is no different from his counterpart in ancient China.